love balcony
and other poems

by Elliot M. Rubin

love balcony
and other poems

Copyright Library of Congress
July2020

ISBN - 978-1-7328493-8-9

cover photo by Andrea Piacqadio from Pexels

Dedication
To my grandchildren
Shane, Isabelle, Jonathan, Carter,
Alexandra, Melanie, Mollie, and Madison

In Memory of my father
Herman S. Rubin
Who wrote poetry all his life.

Preface

Poetry is to be read and understood. To be written in plain language for everyone's enjoyment. Too often, poets write in-depth, penetrating poems where you need to be well-read and versed in the nuances of literature to appreciate the poetry, not this book or any of my writings.

Table of Contents

love balcony

living in manhattan
you never meet neighbors,
until the quarantine
when i met her that day

i walked out on my small
balcony, standing there,
looking down at the street
when i saw her on hers

she smiled and waved to me
i was smitten, in love;
wearing a small bikini
teasing me, jiggling too

i tried to figure out
which apartment is hers-
how can we meet i thought,
then he came out to kiss her

she

she spoke, but no one listened,
they heard but ignored the advice
because it didn't come from a man-
men can be like this, frequently

half the world's population is HER

she is as smart as any male
works as hard if not more
deserves as much pay, plus
the respect for her worth

she has a **he** in **he**r pronoun
plus an extra letter too-
she is a jewel in any crown,
so give her what is rightfully due

beer

speaking about politics
heats up the room -
spittle forms in the corners
of angry lips
defending the indefensible

people are dying
due to incompetence-
lies float in the air;
while talking heads
foment insurrection

good times remembered
as old times years ago-
reality is fake, seniors are
expendable, death helps
the economy, we are doomed

wish i had an ice-cold beer
meeting my friends,
commiserating
on the state of the nation;
while we still have one

wish i had an ice-cold beer

hidden treasures

it will be a treasure hunt
after i'm gone,
looking for my books;
to read them and discover
wonderful poems
the world missed
while i was here

i hope one day
someone will discover
my thoughts and feelings,
so i can live forever
through my writing

although i will be
long gone by then

walk'n and talk'n with God

as i walk down the staircase of life
i'm coming to the final few steps
where i'll end my long tiresome journey;
depression and despair are constant companions
when i hear a gentle voice whispering out to me;
wait and listen, so i did

come walk with me we'll talk a little-
God held my hand i felt so secure;
he gave me the hope i lost long ago;
i listened to words i forgot from my youth

i turned around and walked back up-
God was with me step by step,
never leaving me alone to fall

i walked and talked
a while;
i'm so glad;
i found a way back home

mother

i don't remember her
ever hugging me
or even giving kisses,
yet i know she cared

this past
mother's day
i started
to think about her

in quarantine you
tend to miss
personal touching
from loved ones

i always
hug and kiss
my kids,
the grand ones too

maybe,
it's my way
of compensating?
i don't know

food of love

whipped cream and strawberries
is my favorite treat,
i like to put them in places
where i love to eat

two hot pink cherries
covered in chocolate
waiting to be licked,
i love those small berries

she knows what i like,
served on a shiny satin cotton platter,
it is, of course, the main meal
to me which does matter

lucky tattoo

the chocolate cake looks delicious
as she cuts a petite slice
placing it gingerly on her plate-
the cresting curves of sweet delight
highlight the fire engine red
maraschino cherry sitting atop in all its glory-
lifting her polished silver fork
she places a small sliver of cake
on her tongue, bringing it back
between full pink lips,
slowly savoring the soft frosting,
swishing it from side to side,
waiting to swallow it;
finally sending it down

i am sitting across from her table
watching a small bird tattoo
on her chest, peeking out
from under her unbuttoned white blouse-
not able to stop staring
i saw a small piece of frosting
fall off the fork
landing by the bluebirds beak

i'm jealous;
the bird gets to lick the spot
not i

choices

the early morning sun
peeks in from the sides of
a crisp white linen shade
landing on her young face

long lustrous auburn hair
cascades down on firm breasts
gently spraying out on a taut
youthful stomach

this morning as the dawn shines
through a yellowed wrinkled shade
it wakes me, not her-
i look over to see my wife

her gray hair now cut short
the oxygen mask covering
a still beautiful face, plastic
tubes leading to a green tank

once firm mounds sag to
the side, a tight abdomen
a memory; the love of lust
changed heads, now more mature

remembering good times, kids,
grandkids, i know her journey is
soon over; i question whether
to join her after she leaves

or wait for my eventual ticket

food on the table

sitting on an adirondack chair
at the edge of a rural lake,
gentle waves lap at the shore
lulling me to sleep at dusk

as the sun sets, two boys sit
with a can of freshly dug worms,
fishing rods in hand to catch
one of the lakes big bass fish

with a tug on the line the rod
starts to bend with the reel-spinning-
the clicking sound opens my eyes
to see them excited to scoop their catch
in the net, they laid beside them-
after a short battle, the fish breaks
through the surface standing on its tail
fighting to go free

the hook flies out of its mouth-
it was to be tonight's dinner meal
since both parents are out of work;
with no money left to buy food

lips

i can't help see her face-
full lips glistening
deep-set eyes a sparkle
with a captivating smile

long hair softly resting
on soft velour shoulders,
catching the eyes of men
walking by as she stands here

our fingers interlock, sending
bolts of love through my heart,
though i know the honest truth;
we can only be friends

wealthy men date her, buy
her jewelry, cars, expensive clothes;
we grew up together,
                    i know my place-
then she kissed me,
                    and my world changed

the undressed poet's collection
two poems

parody the codpiece - a Shakespeare parody

also poor Yorick
as Shakespeare once said
he misplaced his codpiece
when he woke from the bed

it was sent out to launder
Lady Macbeth did the wash
t'was the dirty palace lot
she cursed at that damn spot

o codpiece, codpiece
wherefore art though
my jewels doth hang
like bells that do rang

Mercutio and Tybalt
did duel with their swords,
two sabers and two hidden-
only death caused a halt

as she laid down poisoned
on a bed made of fleece
her suitor's not present
he lacks his clean codpiece

Stopping by a Closet on a Snowy Evening - a Frost parody

Whose clothes these are I think I know.
Her house is in the village though
No one will see me undressed here
They're outside watching the falling snow

My girlfriend thinks I'm much too queer
To wear her wig from ear to ear
With bra and girdle, silk stockings too
I'm out of the closet this fine year

My girlfriend gives her head a shake
To ask if there is some mistake
The only sound's one of disbelief
Cause my outfit is so very brief

Her closets lovely, dark and deep,
Now here are clothes I want to keep,
And hours to try on before I sleep
And hours to try on before I sleep

favorite places

favorite place #1

nestled in her arms
kisses on my lower lip
i belong right here

favorite place #2

i saw
   …while standing on the beach in La Jolla
i can smell the salty Pacific Ocean
as it floats in on gentle waves
watching the sunset on the horizon
into the darkened water at dusk
   …the high altitude abandoned
adobe ruins in Colorado after eating
a chuck wagon's iron pan-fried chicken
with the sun beating down
   …the unending, green colored
Great Plains as far as my eyes can see
with my back to the Rocky Mountains
inhaling clean air for the first time
   …the colors of the Southwest in Santa Fe
or visiting artists in Taos New Mexico,
then flying to sin city, Nevada to gamble
while waiting to see star-studded shows
   …Chicago in winter is frigid with winds of ice
blowing in from the great lakes; while summer
in tropical Florida is scorching, tasting sweat if outside
   ...the cool, treed, mountain valleys of Vermont,
tasting sweet fresh maple syrup while making
remarkable
memories of small, quaint New England towns

my favorite place is America

favorite place #3

sitting in the backseat
with her on our first date,
sparks flew, the gates of heaven
opened to send an angel down to earth

she was not the last angel
to be there either, as the skies
were plentiful; luckily i was
able to catch many, as they fell

if a location could write,
a thick book might be written-
so when in old age i think back
i can say the backseat of dad's car

was one of my favorite places

memories

i remember
what your lips are like,
the gentle smile on your face;
sweet words flow like honey
as whispers from your mouth-
all hidden now by a mask;
maybe never seen again
if either of us gets sick

i need your physical touch,
the closeness of your body,
emotions only lovers know-
yes, it is true,
i remember

A Bunker Boy extended limerick

There once was a girl from Nantucket
Married, with kids by the bucket
One's shirt she bent to tuck it
Married Trump* did try to f**k it

Not able to get the girl
Our flag he did unfurl
Holding a bible in his hand up high
To become a dictator, he did try

Peaceful marchers he shot with tear gas
While soldiers protected his white ass
So many girls and boys did protest
He wanted them shot at his behest

The coward hid in the bombproof basement
Soothing missing bone spurs in his feet
While the crowds in front did meet
He sat with burgers and fries to eat

washington

as the dark gray storm clouds
float over the capital, a nation
in shock reels from the election,
feeling darkness approach

grifters and conmen swoop in
grabbing what they could for
friends and themselves; leaving
bare cupboards for folks they serve

ignorance and incompetence rule
as a hundred thousand die 'cause
warnings are ignored, greed runs
rampant; why kill the golden goose?

"i have met the enemy, and they are us."
Pogo said years ago; it applies today too-
vote the incompetents out in November

civil liberties abandoned

Tiananmen Square = Lafayette Square
troops shoot at civilians
peacefully gathered
to petition government
for societal change

the constitution violated,
democracy threatened,
all for a draft-dodging
wannabe dictator
wanting a photo op

Bashō Haiku

Bashō, the master
Always brings outside inside
On paper for you

floral poem

the floral bouquet was over there,
different colors bright and cheery,
some taller, some shorter, depending on stems,
i walked over to pick one out

touching it, i felt softness, tenderness,
an innate beauty i could not resist-
i chose the best flower from the bunch,
then married her for many happy years

nature is diverse

The rose bush
  has sharp thorns
while Rose's red lips
  can bite when speaking-
On a field of green grass
  stands a single yellow daisy
    declaring its lone independence,
while the yellow strands
  of Daisy's hair
    are woven in cornrows
      of teenage rebellion-
The Venus flytrap
  is not what it seems,
nor is Venus
  who is a crossdresser

sacrifice

sacrifice is more than a word of loss,
it is a screaming banner of righteousness
to move toward civility away from hatred
to love thy neighbor no matter skin color
to accept differences as good diversity

love one another as a human being
not less than, but as equals, to
cheer accomplishments of others
if they benefit the world, no matter ethnicity-
sacrifice can be the footstool of a beginning

leaving behind the ills of society

my door

the door, on occasion, will open
allowing in warm emotions,
heating my heart, enabling me
to open arms wide embracing you

sometimes the door closes too;
when you left me, breaking my
heart, leaving it cold and fragile-
brittle, unable to warm up again

since you left, i lost the key-
the door appears to be closed,
there is little i can do-
i need you back to unlock it

footsteps

today i realized
my footsteps
are reminders of my life-
the ones i took
walking down the aisle
to be married,
hastily dashing
down the hall
to see my firstborn child,
the steps of mourning
when my parents died

tracing the footsteps
of my life
is an autobiography

kathy marie

lovers in high school
we never married
due to parent's objections,
cause religions are different-
we now meet
when either has a need;
through the dating of others,
several marriages, divorces
and vacations together
we have come to realize
we are, to each other,
human trampolines

enough

it's time to stop
it's time to talk
it's time to protest
it's time, to be honest

bigotry has run out of time
bigotry has to stop now
bigotry has no basis in fact
bigotry has to be taught

people bleed
people cry
people hurt
people = people

enough killing
enough racism
enough illogic
ENOUGH IS ENOUGH!

insanity

i love you,
for years, i've known you
yet you never said
there is a future for us;
how long can i wait?

we keep talking, going over things;
i have the gun in my hand-
is there someone else?
not sure if i can handle it,
my hand is shaking, nerves brittle

i'm getting tired of this.
mom keeps telling me
to stop speaking into the mirror;
guess i'll have to leave you,
not sure if i am man enough

quarantine

must stay in
can't go out
love to sin
drinking stout

it feels like
three months of
sundays, with
nothing to do!

sunbathing at the beach

naked by the sea
salty breezes wash
over her body,
goosebumps erupting
while elbows burrow
in the sand, supporting
a toned frame-
chest arched high
attracting glances
from young men
eager to approach;
they stop when her lover
leans over to kiss
pink lush lips
on her tanned face-
they walk away
letting the girls
be alone

love lost

i loved you-
yet you left me,
broke my heart

never said why

having a hard time
forgetting you,
i try to move forward

you were my first

somethings in life
are almost impossible
to get over

i'll always remember

goodbye kink hello love

she wore a sheer nightgown
leaving nothing to the imagination,
our relationship is the same,
she always sees right through me

ulterior motives are useless
i can't hide them from her, i did try;
she keeps crawling into my mind
i feel so very bewildered

at last, i broke her magical spell
met a princess who made me her king
i'm out of the dark, dingy dungeon
finally sitting on my royal throne

thought love is a two-way street
each loving the other way more,
she forgot and wanted it all
so I got up, walked out the door

leftovers

it is a small town where
kids all date each other,
some even marry,
except for her

quiet as a church mouse,
friendly, gets along with most
yet never on a date, or kissed,
except by her parents

prom is coming, boys with girls,
gay kids with gay kids,
all excited and accepted
except one girl has no date

on to college, then moves
to the big city, a great job,
a small apartment, still alone
till food shopping one day

reaching for the last milk
in the case, another hand
touches hers, a leftover milk
brought a leftover girl, love

BLM

demonize them-
cause of the nation's problems-
segregate them-
laws to belittle them-
they are dangerous-
do not belong here-
create a climate of hostility towards them-
police attack them-
arrested for just being who they are-
massive imprisonments-

do these apply today?

hate is hard to eradicate-
these were what the Nazis
did to Jews in Germany

i put BLM in the heading.
people = people
different time, different place,
the same discrimination

a mistress' viewpoint

during lunch you gently placed
your hand over mine-
your strength flowed through my
silky soft skin,
melting my resistance
to your motives

i felt the gold ring with diamonds
on the finger next to your wedding band;
did you notice i didn't pull my hand
back from under yours?

i enjoy your company,
our cuddling when we meet-
the hidden moments
your valuable gifts are so lovely

i am young and pert-
if i don't build a nest egg now
it will be too late
when gravity sags my assets,
or the caverns on my face
become too deep
for concealer to fill

i like to travel with you
for business in other cities;
i look forward to leapfrogging
from you to a single
rich daddy-
after all, to be honest,
i'm not the side piece,
you are one of many

fond memories

she is my soulmate-
touching her smooth flesh
is so sensual, titillating;
soft kisses on my lips
are embedded forever
on my memory-
our years together were magical
filled with love and children-
summers in the country when younger,
running through tall fields of grass,
swimming in a small pond
where the creek empties, watching tiny fish
swim and country frogs basking on the banks
sunning themselves while watching us-
her premature death devastates me

virus

the rattle brattle of nurses
hustling into rooms,
patients pushed through busy halls-
doctors listening,
listening,
listening to heartbeats
lungs gasping for air

food service bypassing patient rooms
glucose bags are filling their veins,
plastic tubes going and coming
from all parts of each body

a large hospital with many floors
the pandemic is running amok-
patient rooms are not what they seem;
sadly, they're portals to heaven

remorse

on the side of my parent's driveway
is a long sliver of grass and trees
with the most massive anthill i ever saw;
as a ten-year-old, i had to destroy it

the tiny creatures were nothing to me,
they had no rights to exist or be there,
so i did everything i could to kill them
but they always rebuilt their mounds

i'm seventy-four and remember it well.
this morning i killed a spider in my home;
i felt such remorse after squashing it
my mind sprang back to sunny days of youth

i am driving down the highway of life,
seeing the dark endless tunnel ahead;
now understanding all life is sacred;
forgive me, for i feel guilt over my past

a place in space

in my worldview, there is space,
she met me in a familiar place-
we hit it off, cordoned our own space
others floated around, we stood in place-

a few weeks later, she is in my place
my closet divided into our own space,
I'm thrilled she is in my home place
i have mine, she has a w i d e r space

we love it when we kiss face to face
i am so happy she lives in my place,
with her, i love to share my space

pairs

when i open the closet
i see pairs of my work boots,
except her shoes are now missing

leaving
      space
           for
                memories

fingers

extended hands interlock fingers;
a tactile sensation sends thoughts
prancing through their minds,
waking primal feelings, long-dormant

craving to be wanted again-
missing the giving, the emotions,
the ability to care for someone
more than yourself, or even life itself

the simple act of holding hands
with someone cared for,
releases feelings new to some,
old to others, yet needed by many

anticipation

an old man
sits in a park
on a slat wood bench,
looking at a small pond
while overhead
chicks hatched,
chirping with hunger,
waiting
for their mother to return

years ago
an unwed mother
left her newborn
in the park
wrapped in a blanket
with a note
never to return

for seventy years
on the date
the baby was left,
he returns
hoping his mother,
one day,
will come back
to claim him

halloween introspection

he is still in costume

every day, all-day,
never taking it off

no one sees the real him

love, love, love

upon reflection,
there are many beliefs
the world over
who think their deity
is supreme over others

the question is, which one?

who has the moral high ground
to judge others beliefs,
lifestyles, sexual preferences,
who they can marry?

contrary to religious beliefs,
sexual relations between
consenting adults, in private,
is nobody's business but theirs

in this life, you need to love all,
be kind to everyone you meet,
respect differences in people,
and love, love, love everyone

water

the soft, searing sand of the beach
worms its way through my toes
while i am looking out
at the endless ocean-
so much water everywhere
it is hard to escape from
the never-ending fluid

more than half
earth's surface
is water-
we need it to survive;
most of our body
is water too

but i don't want it in my scotch!

songbird

a songbird
flies overhead,
breathtaking;
wings stretch out
it soars higher
reaches heights
few attain

far below,
the flocks hears
it sing, its voice clear,
strong, powerful
beyond the reach
of others
though they try,
never reaching its glory

at its zenith
it crashes,
dying
in a birdbath-
the flocks gather
in sorrow,
anguish
at the loss of
an unequaled talent
too soon in its life

Goodbye Whitney

poets & poetry

genius is hard to find-
nobody walks around
looking for a poet
to publish and read

no matter how different,
the creative words flow
from the pen
a poet toils alone;
writing impactful poems
stimulating readers
cerebral desires
for literary artistry

those lucky enough
to stumble across
a poet's works
receive a gift
to remain forever
in their soul

the burden of being a poet
is to create, yet be unknown-
it's a dead-end calling, where
only the dead ones are famous

Other books of poetry by Elliot M. Rubin

Scrambled Poems from my Heart
A Boutique Bouquet of Poems and Stories
Rumblings of an Old Man
Surf Avenue Girl - semi episodic poems
Flash Pan Poetry
Unrequited Love
Aliyah - an Episodic Memoir
My Life if I took a Different Path -
        an Episodic Memoire
Bent Twigs and Wet Feet
Stories of the South - semi episodic poems
Selected Poems by Elliot M. Rubin
Chains of Love and other Poems
Cookies and milk with poetry
Paper + pen = poetry

www.CreativeFiction.net

www.ingramcontent.com/pod-product-compliance
Lightning Source LLC
Chambersburg PA
CBHW061656180626
46818CB00003B/1122